Math Monsters

MEASURING

The Perfect Playhouse

Based on the Math Monsters™ public television series, developed in cooperation with the National Council of Teachers of Mathematics (NCTM).

by John Burstein

Reading consultant: Susan Nations, M.Ed., author/literacy coach/consultant
Math curriculum consultants: Marti Wolfe, M.Ed., teacher/presenter; Kristi Hardi-Gilson, B.A., teacher/presenter

WEEKLY WR READER®
EARLY LEARNING LIBRARY

Please visit our web site at: **www.earlyliteracy.cc**
For a free color catalog describing Weekly Reader® Early Learning Library's list
of high-quality books, call 1-877-445-5824 (USA) or 1-800-387-3178 (Canada).
Weekly Reader® Early Learning Library's fax: (414) 336-0164.

Library of Congress Cataloging-in-Publication Data

Burstein, John.
    Measuring: the perfect playhouse / by John Burstein.
        p. cm. — (Math monsters)
    Summary: The four math monsters learn about measurement when they ask
Annie Ant to build a playhouse for them.
        ISBN 0-8368-3813-0 (lib. bdg.)
        ISBN 0-8368-3828-9 (softcover)
        1. Mensuration—Juvenile literature. [1. Measurement.] I. Title.
    QA465.B8974   2003
    530.8—dc21
                                                    2003045041

This edition first published in 2004 by
Weekly Reader® Early Learning Library
330 West Olive Street, Suite 100
Milwaukee, WI 53212 USA

Text and artwork copyright © 2004 by Slim Goodbody Corp. (www.slimgoodbody.com).
This edition copyright © 2004 by Weekly Reader® Early Learning Library.

Original Math Monsters™ animation: Destiny Images
Art direction, cover design, and page layout: Tammy Gruenewald
Editor: JoAnn Early Macken

Printed in the United States of America

1 2 3 4 5 6 7 8 9 07 06 05 04 03

You can enrich children's mathematical experience by working with
them as they tackle the Corner Questions in this book. Create
a special notebook for recording their mathematical ideas.

Measurement and Math

Measurement is one of the most widely used of mathematical skills.
It bridges two main areas of math, geometry
and the use of numbers.

Meet the Math Monsters™

ADDISON

Addison thinks
math is fun.
"I solve problems
one by one."

Mina flies
from here to there.
"I look for answers
everywhere."

MINA

MULTIPLEX

Multiplex
sure loves to laugh.
"Both my heads
have fun with math."

Split is friendly
as can be.
"If you need help,
then count on me."

SPLIT

We're glad you want to take a look
at the story in our book.

We know that as you read, you'll see
just how helpful math can be.

Let's get started. Jump right in!
Turn the page, and let's begin!

    The Math Monsters were outside. They were playing
ball, having fun, and singing a song.
    "We play outside in the spring and fall.
    We catch and throw and bounce a ball.
    We roll it far. We kick it high
    and watch it fly into the sky."
    The monsters looked up. They saw a dark rain cloud
coming near.

"Run," said Split, "or we will all get wet."

"We will have to play inside today," said Multiplex.

What games do you like to play when it is raining?

The monsters were safe and dry inside. Addison said,
"If we build a playhouse, we can play ball even on rainy
days."

"Good idea," said Multiplex. "Let's call Annie Ant.
She is a builder."

The monsters called her.

"Hello," said Annie Ant. "How can I help you?"

The monsters told her all about the playhouse.

"How big do you want it?" asked Annie.

"Sort of long," said Addison.

"Kind of wide," said Split.

"Nice and tall," said Mina.

Will this information tell Annie all she needs to know?

"I do not know what you mean," said Annie.

"When you say sort of long, how long is that? When you say kind of wide, how wide is that? When you say nice and tall, how tall is that? Please go outside and measure the size you want. Then call me back."

When the rain stopped, the monsters went outside to measure. They called Annie back.

"We want the playhouse to be as long as the space between the apple tree and the rosebush," said Split.

"We want it as wide as the space between the rosebush and the swing," said Addison.

"We want it as tall as the second branch on the apple tree," said Mina.

Is this the information Annie needs?

"I have never seen your rosebush, your swing, or your apple tree," said Annie. "I still do not know how big you want your playhouse to be. I need numbers — real numbers! Please measure it again."

"We have to find a better way to measure," said Mina.

Can you think of a way to measure so Annie gets the numbers she needs?

"I will pace it out," said Addison. "I will put one foot in front of the other, heel to toe."

"I will count the number of steps you take. I will write the numbers down," said Split.

When they were done, Multiplex called Annie back. He said, "Here are the numbers. We want our playhouse to be 100 steps long, 60 steps wide, and 30 steps high."

"That is much better," said Annie. "I will build it today."

Why does Annie think this information is better?

Annie and her carpenter ants came to the castle. The monsters were away at a birthday party.

"OK, workers," said Annie. "The monsters are away, but we can still build their playhouse. I know they want the playhouse to be 100 steps long, 60 steps wide, and 30 steps high. I can pace it out for myself."

Annie paced it out, one ant foot in front of the other. She started to build.

When the monsters came home, they found a big surprise!

What do you think the monsters saw?

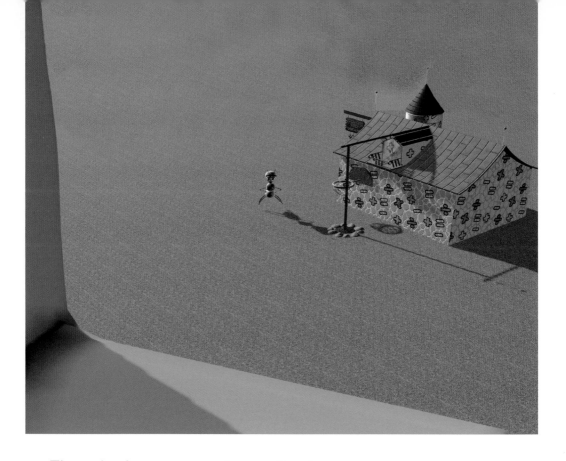

The playhouse was teeny-tiny!

"What have you done?" asked Split. "The playhouse you built is too small. We will never fit inside."

Annie looked up. She said, "I used the numbers you gave me. It is 100 steps long, 60 steps wide, and 30 steps high."

If Annie used the monsters' numbers, what went wrong?

"We measured with Addison's monster step," said Multiplex.

"I measured with my ant step," said Annie.

"Your step is much smaller than mine," said Addison.

"I can fix it," said Annie.
"All I need to know is the size
of Addison's step."

What can the monsters do to show Annie Ant the size of Addison's step?

"Let's trace my foot on a piece of paper," said
Addison. "Then we will know the size of my step."

The monsters traced Addison's foot on paper. Mina cut it out. She gave it to Annie.

"This is a great tool," Annie said. "I will use it from now on."

How will this tool help Annie?

Annie used Addison's step to measure. This time, the playhouse was just the right size.

"Thank you, Annie," said the monsters.

"You are welcome," Annie said. "From now on, I will ask everyone to use a copy of Addison's step to measure what they want me to build. That way, we will all agree on the size."

The monsters went inside their playhouse.
They were so happy, they sang a song.
"We love our playhouse, long and wide,
with lots of room to play inside.
We love our playhouse, big and tall,
with room to throw or kick a ball.
Now we have a place to play
when it is a rainy day."

What other tools do people use to measure things?

ACTIVITIES

Page 5 Everyday games are filled with mathematics. The next time children play with cards, building blocks, clay, or dice, talk with them about the connections to math.

Page 7 Talk with children about the kinds of jobs carpenters do. Try role-playing and "hire" children to build a structure out of blocks. Discuss what information they'll need to do the job.

Page 9 Discuss how approximations often don't provide enough information. For example, suppose someone went to a clothing store and asked for pants that were sort of long and a shirt that was kind of big. Ask children to explain why they think this is not enough information for Annie to build a playhouse.

Pages 11, 13 Explore ways to measure the distance between two places using numbers. For example, you can count the number of steps, blocks, wire hangers, or clothespins. Use objects of uniform length and keep a record of the measurements.

Page 15 Have children make a prediction and explain their reasoning.

Page 17 Ask children to compare the size of their hands to yours. Then ask them to explain what they think went wrong in making measurements for the playhouse.

Pages 19, 21 Ask children to trace one hand on paper and cut it out. Then ask them to count how many hand lengths it takes to cross a table.

Page 23 Take a trip to the hardware store to look at measuring tools.